RANDOLPH

Written by
Eric Copeland

Cover Illustration by Andria "Dria" Copeland

PAGE PUBLISHING
Conneaut Lake, PA

First originally published by Page Publishing 2024

ISBN 979-8-88654-695-8 (pbk)
ISBN 979-8-88654-708-5 (hc)
ISBN 979-8-88654-701-6 (digital)

Printed in the United States of America

INTRODUCTION

Many generations ago, before the story of Rudolph, there lived in the North Pole another set of reindeer. They were known as the Brown Skins. They lived a life that would be unbearable to most in the animal kingdom. They were underappreciated most of the time even though they had done the majority of the work for many years, but were never considered equal to those other reindeer. Unlike those other reindeer, the Brown Skins were unable to fly; they were labeled as handicapped by the others. It was only during the Christmas season when they felt included as peers, and that was mostly because of their need to help with the workload of the Christmas preparations. Many of the elders discussed their anger and hurt among themselves in private for fear of retaliation from the other reindeer. The Brown Skins lived a simple life, yet they were extremely intelligent. They shared many things as a family, and most of the time, their immediate survival depended on the elders providing for them. The Christmas season, as we know it, has been written about the North Pole many times. The stories of the Brown Skins were left out intentionally, leaving a one-sided story from the very beginning. This is the story of Randolph and the Brown Skin reindeer.

1

It was Christmas Eve, with the usual chaos at that time of year. Months before Christmas, the elders gathered together to discuss what they could do about the future of the Brown Skins. They didn't want any more generations to suffer the hardships of being in the north with the other reindeer. They had to make a choice in order to survive and continue to exist as a community with its own culture. They all looked up to the eldest Brown Skin. His name was Randolph. He was their leader. Randolph and a few of the other elders decided that the only way for the Brown Skins to achieve their own destiny was to relocate to another region, but they knew if the other reindeer found out, it would lead to a future of extreme conditions and more separation from what they had been taught by the ancestors. They knew the other North Pole reindeer could be ruthless at times. A decision was made that when Santa began his annual trip with toys for the kids, it would be the perfect time to start their migration. They didn't know where it would lead them or how long it would take, but they knew it would be a difficult journey; many had never left the confines of their homes. The Brown Skins were very adaptable and could survive in any type of weather conditions, especially the snow. They would use the fierce winter storm as their cover so they wouldn't be detected at the time of their departure. The children were not told about what would happen because Randolph decided only the elders should know about their plans.

2

As the evening began to fall, everyone did their usual duties: loading the sleigh, clearing a path for the takeoff, and making sure the fat man in the red suit had everything that he needed for a safe trip around the globe and a safe return trip home. A feast was prepared by Momma Sophia. She was Randolph's life partner. They had been together for over forty years. Sophia had been preparing the Christmas feast for many years, but she couldn't remember how long she had been doing it. It was passed on to her by her ancestors. All she knew was that everyone looked forward to her Christmas Eve feast. The Brown Skins were not allowed to eat in the main dining quarters with the others, but they served the food and drinks. The children were allowed to mingle but only under the supervision of the elders of the other reindeer. The children also had to eat in the designated section for the Brown Skins, but they didn't understand why. Randolph informed the elders that the migration would begin with the onslaught of the blizzard that was in the forecast.

3

Snow began falling at the end of the feast. Large snowflakes were making visibility so thick it would be virtually impossible for anyone to see them leave. With the blizzard, they couldn't see more than a few feet at a time, perfect conditions for the Brown Skins to start their migration. Santa used the cover of darkness to leave the North Pole to keep out of sight the Burgermiesters, a radical group who hated the Christmas season and never celebrated it. They had done all they could to defeat the joy of the season. Sophia wanted to make sure she had gathered all of her recipes; they had been passed down from generation to generation. Sophia treasured those recipes with all of her heart. They were special to her, and she looked forward to passing them on to future generations. The recipes also contained a formula for brewing a special tea made with leaves that were only found in the North. She believed the tea had special powers and was used for many things, including healing the Brown Skins from different ailments and protecting them from many diseases. It also contained a secret ingredient that allowed the elders of the Brown Skins to fly for fifteen to thirty minutes. They were only allowed to drink it during the Christmas season. Sophia kept the secret formula in her head. She didn't disclose it to anyone; not even Randolph or her three sisters knew what the mixture was. The other reindeer made it illegal for the Brown Skins to drink it at any other time.

4

The time had arrived for the migration to begin. Randolph and a few of the elders had charted a map that would lead them away from the North Pole. They would start the migration by going south because every year, the birds would fly south just before the big freeze in the north, but they would always return with the warm weather, and the elders agreed to follow the map drawn up by Randolph and the others. Some were concerned because of the severity of the winter storm that was approaching. The elders assured everyone that everything would just be fine, and the migration began. Several days passed before they decided to take a rest. The children were getting restless and had begun to question their parents about why they left the North Pole and were told they were searching for a new area to call home, but they didn't understand. What had started out as a few days had now turned into several months, but the migration kept going south. Randolph sent out a scout crew consisting of a family of eagles whom

Randolph had befriended many years before the migration had entered into his mind. The eagle family assisted the Brown Skins many times when they were gathering food at the North Pole. They had a very unique technique of gauging the wind direction, and they could predict the weather several days before it approached. They were the ones who helped Randolph plan the start of the migration by forecasting the snowstorm that would come on Christmas Eve. Randolph had complete confidence in them, especially his long-time friend elder Eyes Eagle. They had been friends since childhood, and their bond was unbreakable.

5

What had begun as a migration that many thought would last only a couple of weeks had now turned into several months of constant moving from territory to territory with those months accumulating to years. The Brown Skins continued the tradition of the Christmas season. The elders changed the name to the festive season to help erase the brutal memories of living in the north with the other reindeer. It had now been almost five years since the beginning of the migration, and the Brown Skins hadn't found a place to call home. Some of the Brown Skins began to question Randolph's leadership and decided to leave the migration and search for a new home on their own, even though the elders insisted that they remain together. Randolph was getting up in age, and his health had begun to fail. He told Sophia that he did not want the other elders to know how sick he had become because he would have to give up this leadership role if he became ill, which had been agreed upon by Randolph and the elders before the start of the migration. The

Brown Skins created a leadership council during the migration to help with keeping law and order. Many of the children who began the migration as youngsters were now older along with Randolph's and Sophia's children. Their oldest son, Claude, was being groomed for a leadership position. They didn't have any daughters. Claude was much older than his brothers. He was the split image of his father, and he had always been a natural leader, even as a child. Claude knew his father was sick and his health was fading fast. He swore to his father that he would make sure the great migration would be completed, but he wasn't sure if when his time came to lead, the others would continue to follow him. Randolph told Claude about a dream that he had: they had found a home in his dream, and the place he saw had beautiful trees, but there was something unique about their branches that made them stand out like a broom, and also in this dream, he remembered seeing ice mountains. Claude thought the tea may have made his father hallucinate, but Sophia said she hadn't made any tea. The climate in the north wouldn't allow trees to grow because of the harsh conditions. The temperatures rarely rose above freezing, leaving all vegetation to be grown inside, which was some of the duties of the Brown Skins.

6

Randolph organized a secret meeting with the leadership council to inform them about the condition of his health. He asked them what they would do if by chance he was to pass away and who would take over his role in leading the migration. Many of the elders on the council were also up in age with their own health issues. Randolph insisted that they make the new leadership role the number one priority because he wanted the migration to continue. Randolph knew they could not return to the North Pole because of how they left. The council decided to meet again in three days to talk about who would be chosen as the new leader of the Brown Skins. They were concerned about Randolph and his health. Randolph had lost a tremendous amount of weight, and he always had a powerful voice, but his voice was almost at a whisper. Sophia went with Randolph on a walk after the meeting. Along the way, they saw Claude. Randolph called out to him to have a conversation. He needed to inform Claude about the meeting with the elders, but he had a lot of trouble with these words. Claude also had his son with him. His name was Pierre, and just like his father, he too resembled his grandfather. Randolph loved his grandson and enjoyed his company. He would always tell Sophia how smart Pierre was as a small child. He was gifted and had a photographic memory. Randolph told Claude about his illness and the meeting he had with the elders. He told Claude he was going to nominate him for the leadership roles in the migration. Claude told him that he wasn't ready to lead, but Randolph told him that he would not take no for an answer and the other elders would have to agree before he could assume the leadership role. Sophia reminded Claude of the many times he took charge of the family when Randolph left with the work crew while they were at the North Pole. Finally Claude agreed but only if the council voted for him with a unanimous vote, and Randolph agreed. Pierre followed his grandmother back to where they had taken shelter for the night. Eyes Eagle notified the council about an approaching storm and also the big water they saw while they were on scout patrol. He told them that the migration was about two days away from the big water, but the storm was approaching quickly.

7

The council gathered on the third day as planned. They all wrote a name on a small piece of paper with the name of whom they had chosen. Randolph asked Eyes Eagle to join them and read aloud the name on each member's paper. There were seven in the council, including Randolph. The number seven was chosen, so there wouldn't be a tie. It would give the leader the opportunity to cast the last vote. Eyes read each note one at a time. It was a unanimous vote; all of the elders voted for Claude to become the next leader of the migration. Randolph became overwhelmed with emotions. All he could think about was that he had lived long enough to see Claude inherit the torch for generations to come. He knew Claude would be an outstanding leader, and he couldn't wait to give him and Sophia the good news. Once he told Sophia, she informed her sisters about the special occasion, and they planned a big feast and celebration. Claude was grateful and committed that he would make all of them proud and asked for his father to hold on just a little longer; he would see those trees and ice mountains soon. Claude gave the good news to his life mate. Her name was Abigail, but everyone called her Gabby because she had the gift of gab. She could talk your head off, and she could sing. The elders said she had the voice of an angel. She also had five sisters, and when they all sang together, it was something special. All of the young ladies loved her and looked up to her, and according to the traditions of the Brown Skins, Sophia was supposed to hand over the recipes to Abigail at the leadership ceremony, but she told Randolph she didn't trust Abigail with the recipes, especially the tea formula, because of her gift of gab and her five sisters. One of Abigail's sisters, in particular, was always confrontational. She was the eldest, and Abigail was the youngest, but Abigail looked up to her because they had lost their mother while Gabby was just a baby, and none of her sisters knew who their father was; he simply disappeared in the middle of the night. Randolph agreed with Sophia to hold on to the recipes for now. Once Sophia explained to Claude the situation, he agreed also.

8

As the ceremonies began, all of those in the migration came to show their support for Claude. Abigail and her sisters opened the ceremony with a beautiful tribute to Randolph. It brought tears to his eyes. Pierre sat with his grandmother. She whispered to him that one day he would become the leader of the Brown Skins, but he didn't understand because he was only a child. All of the elders lined up to ordain Claude as their leader. Claude stepped to the podium and gave his speech. He spoke with authority. He made a promise that all of the Brown skins would have a place to call home soon. He told them not to give up and to keep moving forward and to continue to trust that migration just as their ancestors had done. Claude displayed great compassion for his elders. As he was speaking, Pierre jumped out of his grandmother's lap and ran up to the podium with his father. It brought much laughter from those in attendance. Claude could see his parents sitting on the front row. He noticed his father began to clutch his chest, and it appeared he was in tremendous agony. All of the elders immediately rushed to Randolph to assist him, but he could not be comforted. Sophia became very emotional as she called out to Randolph.

9

What started as a great day with a ceremony took a turn for the worse. Randolph joined the ancestors; he was gone. No one could celebrate. Sophia demanded for everyone to leave her with Randolph. Claude insisted that he would stay with her, but she told him what she needed him to do. Pierre hadn't seen death before and was trying to wake up his grandpa. Sophia tried to explain to him as best she could that his grandpa had left to be with the angels, but he was too young to understand. Abigail took Pierre away, holding him in her arms. It was traumatic for everyone. All Gabby could think about was the night she lost her mother. Even though she was only a baby at that time, she never forgot the sounds of the screams from her sisters. Claude comforted Sophia as best he could, but Sophia kept insisting that he go on and do what she asked. The culture of the Brown Skins required certain things to take place immediately upon the death of an elder. He proceeded to follow her instructions. All of the elders of the council went with him because this would be his first experience as a leader involving the death of an elder. The body of Randolph had to be preserved according to the customs of the Brown Skins. Randolph had been the leader for a very long time, and the elders had to choose a proper burial that would be fit for a king. Eyes Eagle suggested that the elders bury Randolph facing the big water. Sophia agreed because that would allow all of the Brown Skins to pay their final respects. The migration had more than tripled in size from its beginning. Preparations were made for the following day, and all of Sophia's friends and sisters helped in some type of way. They all spent the night with her along with Abigail's eldest sister.

10

As the final service was about to begin, Claude noticed that others who were not a part of the migration had joined them; they were dear friends of Eyes Eagle. They all lined up in a single file and paid their respects to Randolph, each one giving a gift to Sophia. She was moved to tears by the compassion of strangers. It gave her hope that better days would come. Abigail sang a solo; she sang Randolph's and Sophia's favorite song ("There's a Bright Side Somewhere"). Everyone applauded her when she concluded with a personal tribute to Randolph. She spoke about how he always uplifted her and showed her much respect even though she and her sisters were poor and homeless when she first met Randolph. She spoke about how he always joked with her that one day, she would become a queen, and as she began to sob, she fainted and had to be consoled. No one knew she was pregnant, not even Claude. Sophia's eldest sister's name was Margaret. She was the midwife for the Brown Skins. Margaret recognized immediately why Abigail had fainted; she shouted as loud as she could that Abigail was with a child, which in turn brought a great cheer from those who had surrounded her. Sophia didn't know what all the noise was about, but when she found out, it made her extremely happy. She knew it was a blessing, and she knew it was Randolph, letting her know that he was all right and was with the ancestors. Claude didn't know he would have a second child. He and Abigail wanted a daughter to complete their family. He wanted to give the baby Abigail's mother's name, but Abigail refused. She told Randolph that she wanted the baby's name to honor Randolph, but Claude told her it would be silly to give a girl a man's name, and they both laughed.

Then Gabby said to him, "How do you know it's a girl?" and they laughed even harder. Claude thought about his father. He told Sophia that he knew this father was in the mist because he could feel his spirit, and they began the preparations for Randolph's final resting place.

The transition of Randolph into the ancestors took place at the site that Eyes Eagle had suggested. In the foreground, you could see where the land made some type of transition. The site was about a two-day hike from the big water, and it had a beautiful view of the sunrise. Randolph loved to watch the sunrise in the morning. He was an early riser. He used to tell Claude all the time that the morning was the most peaceful time of the day. Claude knew his father would have loved the site Eyes had chosen. Eyes asked his friend Baldly Eagle if he would honor the family by doing a special fly over during the ceremony. He told him it would be the perfect way to honor his lifelong friend. Baldy agreed to perform the flyover, but he reminded Eyes about the fast-approaching storm. Eagles usually don't fly during a storm, so they had to come up with a plan B just in case the storm was too severe. As the ceremony began, the storm became furious, with the wind blowing extremely hard. Baldy did the flyover for his friend. The ceremony lasted for about two hours, and then they all said their final goodbyes, Sophia being the last to speak. She spoke with tears in her eyes and had to be pulled away from Randolph. It was a moving experience for everyone. The migration continued late into the night. Claude wanted to reach the big water with some daylight remaining because no one in the migration had ever seen the big water other than Eyes Eagle.

11

As the morning sun began to rise, Claude was awakened by Eyes Eagle. Eyes told him that they were very close to the water and should arrive within a couple of hours. The news traveled quickly throughout the migrants and brought a well-deserved renewal of fresh energy among everyone; they had just gone through the death of Randolph. Sophia wanted to get the first glimpse of the big water. She was so excited. The first thing they all noticed was how large the big water was; it was so massive that no one could see where it ended. There wasn't any way they could go across the big water for the fear of losing the children and many of the elders. Their only other option was to follow along the shoreline to reach the other side. Claude asked Eyes if he would take his scout crew and follow the shoreline to see where it would lead them. Eyes didn't hesitate and got right on it. Claude and the elders on the council watched him and his crew disappear into the horizon. It was a beautiful day with the sky clear of any clouds.

The weather had changed, and it had a muggy and damp feeling to it. Sophia was amazed at the sight of the big water. She took Pierre to the shore edge with her. She wanted to taste the water and told Claude the water had a salty taste to it, and while she was tasting the water, something came up out of the water, looked at her and Pierre, then disappeared back underneath the surface. Sophia told Claude she hadn't ever seen anything that big move that fast. Claude wondered aloud what it might have been. Eyes Eagle and his crew were gone for several days, more than a week. Claude and the elders began to worry about Randolph's friend. Some thought to themselves that they may have gone back to the north because of the unusual climate. Claude was confident they would return with possibly some good news. The next morning, all of the elders went to the shore to see what came up out of the water and looked at Sophia, but she didn't go with them because she was afraid. They all stood for hours, but nothing came to the shoreline except for a few fish. One of the many blessings the Brown Skins had was that they could interpret other languages. Claude asked one of the fish if he knew of a large creature that lived in the big water. He said that it was probably a whale and they didn't have anything to worry about because the whale was big and a gentle giant. The fish told Claude that the whales saw some folks at the edge of the shore. It was about that time that the kids started cheering loudly because they saw Eyes and his crew coming back across the sky.

When the fish saw Eyes coming, he yelled, "EAGLES," and all the fish vanished underneath the water in a split second; they were terrified. Eyes told Claude he had good news. He told him that they were only a few days from a place that he thought would make a beautiful home for the Brown Skins. He described it to the elders in great detail of what he and the crew had seen. He told them about the trees that had branches and leaves that resembled a broom. When he said that, it got Claude's undivided attention, and he wanted to know what else Eyes had seen. Eyes told him that one side was green with fruit and vegetables along with soft dirt the color of gold and the other side was large mountains made out of ice.

Claude said, "ICE!" And then he ran back to where Sophia was located and told her what Eyes had seen. He knew his grandfather had told him about a dream he had had before his death. Sophia did a dance because she became overwhelmed with joy. Pierre didn't understand, so he began to dance with this grandma, and those around him began to dance and shout with them. Claude made the decision to continue the migration immediately, and they did.

12

The Brown Skins arrived at the location that was described by Eyes Eagle. It had beautiful trees, lakes, and ice mountains. Claude remembered the dream Randolph had spoken about before he crossed over to the ancestors. It was strange that the location with the ice mountains had snow identical to the snow in the north, but in the area that Claude and the others were at, everything was green with beautiful lakes. Claude knew this was going to be the location they would call home. Their arrival also coincided with the festive season, which was only a few weeks away. It would be their first in their new village that they named Brownsville. The children would finally be able to have a safe and enjoyable time. Pierre began to grow and became much stronger than most of the boys his age. He reminded everyone so much of his grandfather. Everyone knew he would follow in his father's footsteps and continue the legacy because he was a natural leader, and in the future, he would assume the leadership role for the Brown Skins.

The women started preparing for the festivities as soon as everyone got settled in. The area was large, and the council gave each family an opportunity to choose the location where they wanted to live. Sophia chose the section that overlooked the big water. She wanted to face the direction where Randolph had been laid to rest. Claude chose the section where the trees were located that Randolph had described in his dream. It was beautiful, and Abigail loved it. She told Randolph that she felt safe and at home in their new village. Gabby selected a secluded section for her garden. She had always talked about having a garden with flowers and fresh vegetables. Sophia thought it was a great idea and she could help Gabby with the garden and plant some herbs for the festive season. It was impossible to grow anything in the north with the climate the way it was. Gabby remembered one of her aunts would talk about the old times and her grandmother's flower garden. Sophia needed special herbs to make her secret tea formula. She asked Claude if he could send someone to search for what she needed. Eyes volunteered immediately because he wanted to see more of the land and he wanted to find a location to live in for his crew and his family.

13

Eyes returned with the special herbs Sophia requested to make her special tea and informed the council that they were not alone; there was another family who were also living in the village. He wasn't sure how long they had been there but it was an elder couple, but it appeared they didn't have any children, but he wasn't sure. Claude insisted that the council should meet them to find out if they were friendly. Eyes led them to where he had seen them last. Once they arrived, it took a few minutes before they became friends. They were very large folks but were very humbled and excited to meet the Brown Skins. Claude invited them back to the village to the rest of the Brown Skins. Their name was the Bears, and the elder name was Paul Bear. He introduced his life mate, and her name was Polaria Bear, and they told him they had been there for several years alone. Paul warned Claude about the night people who never came out during the day and how strange they acted, but they were not hostile in any way.

Sophia wanted a kitchen built, so her sisters could begin to prepare for the feast that was needed for the festive season. She also needed a lot of privacy to prepare the secret tea.

14

bigail told Sophia she felt as if she was having contractions and her baby was coming. Claude and some of the young men built them a beautiful home with multiple rooms. It would be the first time Pierre would have his own room, but he wanted to spend the festive season with his grandma. He loved his grandma, and she enjoyed his curiosity. All she would say is "That boy sure loves his grandma's cooking." Pierre would eat whatever she prepared. He would watch her every move to the very last detail. Every now and then, she would give him a small sip of the tea before she added the key secret ingredient. The next morning, to the delight of everyone, Abigail gave birth to a beautiful baby girl. Pierre picked out her name and called her Joyce because she brought so much joy to the Brown Skins. He was thrilled to finally have a sibling. Sophia had her first and only granddaughter. Baby Joyce had her grandmother's beautiful gray eyes. Pierre said her eyes looked like stars shining at night. He loved his little sister. Joyce was the first baby born in the new village and during the festive season. Sophia reminded everyone that she needed to get back to preparing the special tea and took Baby Joyce with her even though she wasn't two hours old. Baby Joyce filled the void in Sophia's heart that was left with the passing of Randolph. Abigail didn't dare to interrupt. About that time, they heard another scream. It was Polaria. She was giving birth to her and Paul's first child but didn't know she was pregnant. She had always been a fairly large woman. Paul was completely surprised. He was finally going to be a dad. He had given up hope because they were so far gone in age. They didn't have any relatives to celebrate with, which was sad, but Claude told him the Brown Skins were his family now. They did a toast with the council to make it official.

15

This festive season would be Pierre's and his friend's last as juveniles and their antlers began to grow, which signaled the arrival of them becoming young men, and as a part of the Brown Skins' tradition, young males who were reaching puberty could choose their festive gift regardless of what it was. This is how many of the young men selected their life mate, but Pierre wanted to do something different because most of the life mate partnerships rarely lasted until the next festive season. He felt like he and his friends were too young to make that kind of decision at that age. Claude told him that any changes to their customs would have to be approved by the council with a unanimous vote. He and his friends would have to present it to the elders. Claude asked them what changes they wanted to be considered. Pierre told him they all wanted to reshape their antlers instead of growing up and out like the rest of the males. They wanted their antlers to have a twist added to them, which would allow them to grow straight down (dread antlers). Claude organized the meeting with the council to take place later that same evening. The boys selected Pierre to speak on their behalf. It would be his first time in a leadership role, and he loved it. Claude told him he was a natural leader. Pierre reminded the elders so much of his grandfather. He had his grandfather's voice. The elders said Pierre sounded like Randolph speaking from the grave. The council granted the boys' request and made it an official part of their culture. Sophia's eldest sister knew how to do the dreads. She used a special oil that caused them to get soft, which made them easy to twist. She had always wanted to have her own shop. She figured by doing the boys, she would be able to showcase her talent for the others to see. Sophia was happy for her sister. She finally had an opportunity to do what she loved to do, and perhaps it could turn into a profitable business.

16

The Brown Skins celebrated the festive season in their usual fashion. Everyone exchanged gifts with each other, just as they had done in the north. The man in the red suit never paid them a visit in the north, so they were used to doing it their way. Sophia saved the tea for last. It has always been the highlight of the season. The children laughed at their elders who were trying to fly. Some never got off the ground, which made it that much more hilarious. Some of the elders performed acrobatics, and some raced back and forth across the sky until the tea had worn off. The reindeer of the north didn't know about the special tea. It was kept away from their knowledge by the elders because they would have considered it a threat to their culture. The festivities ended on the last Sunday of the twelfth month with the eldest member of the council sharing memories of past times. Storytelling was a source of entertainment for the Brown Skins. It allowed the kids to hear stories about their ancestors and elders to have fond memories of days gone by. In this season, the kids, during the evening when the elders spoke about the past, they learned about Randolph. Many were born after his passing. They learned how he had been a great leader and architect of the great migration. The elders also spoke about the time they lived in the north. Paul Bear told the elders that he had relatives that lived in the north, but he hadn't seen them in such a long time. He wasn't sure if they were still alive, but he knew he would see them again one day. This was Paul's and Polaria's first festive season. They were happy to be a part of the Brown Skins' celebration, but no one could get Paul to drink the tea. He had been afraid of heights since early childhood. He fell out of a tree when he was five years old, and ever since then, anything over four feet high has been off limits. Polaria often teased about it. She would tell him that he was the only bear in the world who wouldn't climb a tree. As time moved forward, Brownsville had become a modernized city, thriving with a robust economy. Its population continued the traditions and culture of the ancestors. Their native language took on an island tone. Everyone seemed to start speaking the same language, and it added to their culture. Pierre had grown into a statue of a man. He resembled his grandfather and had many of the leadership qualities of Claude and his grandfather, Randolph. Sophia was up in age. No one knew exactly how old she was, there weren't any written records, but she continued to be as ornery as ever. Claude also was getting up in age and soon would have to retire. His leadership role would need to be filled by one of the elders. The new generation of children referred to him as Poppa Claude. Pierre found himself a life mate. Her name was Celesta. Sophia loved her because she was a throwback in her mentality and self-esteem. Sophia said Celesta had an old soul. Celesta loved to cook, and she assisted Sophia with all the festive activities.

17

Pierre and Celesta decided to have a family, and she gave birth to twins, a girl and a boy. Pierre named his daughter, Halo, because she had a white circle shaped birthmark on top of her head, and he named his son, Randolph, in honor of his grandfather. Everyone said Baby Randolph had the same facial features as his great-grandfather, and Sophia agreed. Pierre spoke to Celesta, and once the babies were older, it would be the best time for them to go on a vacation. Paul Bear had shown him a section in the ice mountains that was perfect for a getaway. It was secluded but not far from the village. He assured Pierre that the children would be fine and not to worry. He told him to enjoy his vacation. Pierre brought in a construction crew to install a modernized interior that gave it all the comforts of home. It was a surprise for Celesta. She always spoke about a cabin in the snow and ice mountains. He also convinced his grandma to make them a batch of the special tea to take with them on vacation. Sophia made enough tea for them to take about four or five good flights. Halo asked her mother if she could invite her cousin Jean to stay with her while they were on vacation. Sophia wanted to stay also. Jean was Sophia's great niece. She loved to spend time with Halo. They sang all night until the stars disappeared. Pierre and Celesta were having the time of their lives. They toured every inch of the ice mountain. The section Pierre had constructed for Celesta was created with royalty in mind. Pierre suggested they spend the night at the cabin. It was higher in elevation and would give them a view of Brownsville with a breathtaking view of the big water and ice mountains in the background. As they fell asleep, there was a sudden crash that sounded more like an explosion. Pierre reached for his wife, but her body was motionless. Another explosion occurred but missed them by about ten feet. Pierre screamed for Celesta to wake up, but she was gone. He sobbed mightily. His only option was to survive. He drank three bottles of the tea and ran along the shore until he was able to gain flight. He flew out into the big water so he could hide behind the clouds. The three bottles of tea gave him extra speed, and he disappeared in a flash.

18

Spring finally has arrived. Randolph was showing his friends how fast he could run, and in the midst of his running, he began to fly. No one knew he could fly. His friends couldn't believe what they were seeing. They thought he may have drunk a portion of Sophia's tea. They told Claude that Randolph had drunk the secret tea and was flying, but Randolph insisted he did not drink the tea and had always been able to fly but he never told anyone. He told them he finally felt free to not have to keep his gift a secret any longer. Everyone was happy, but there were some who questioned who he was. Pierre and Celesta were expected back later that evening from their vacation. Halo couldn't wait to tell her parents about Randolph's being able to fly. She knew they wouldn't believe her.

Darkness had begun to fall, and Pierre and Celesta had not arrived. Claude began to worry and asked Eyes Eagle to go out and look for them. Paul Bear located the path he used to show

Pierre. The ice mountain was their starting point. Randolph wanted to go with them on the search for his parents, but Poppa Claude would not allow him to go. It was getting darker by the second. Paul and Eyes had special night vision the same as the Brown skins. The search continued throughout the night until dawn. Paul found footprints that led to the shoreline and backtracked the steps to the cabin. They both were shaken by what they saw next. It was the body of Celesta. They recognized her clothing. Her head had been detached from her body. It was extremely traumatic for the both of them. They wrapped her lifeless body in a blanket that Celesta had brought. It was her favorite blanket. They both cried for her. They took her back to the village. It was unbearable news for all to see. Randolph was allowed to see his mother's corpse, but Halo refused. She held on to her great-grandmother Sophia. She cried and screamed for hours. Randolph held his mother's lifeless body, promising to her that he would find out who had done this, even though he was still only a child. He was able to calm Halo for only a moment. She continued to weep openly.

The entire community was devastated with the news of Pierre and Celesta. Pierre's body was never found. Everyone assumed he was killed and then eaten by the night creatures. The only things they found were the three empty bottles of tea and footprints along the shoreline. Claude told everyone that he thought there was a chance for Pierre to be alive and would not stop believing until his son's body was found. He wanted the search to continue for Pierre. Grandma Sophia was over one hundred years old and suffered from dementia. She didn't fully comprehend what had happened. She kept asking for Randolph. She wanted to tell him something. She whispered to him that she loved him. Randolph screamed and cried very loudly, but Sophia didn't understand why he reacted that way, and she became sad.

The ceremony held for Celesta was beautiful. A painting of Celesta was put on display in her honor.

19

fter all of the excitement had subdued, Claude was notified a new family had arrived to the village. They were tired and hungry. Claude asked them where they came from and who they were. The man identified himself by telling Claude his name was Jacque and his life mate's name was Clarissa. They came from a town about twenty miles east of the village because they were in danger, but he didn't elaborate on what kind of danger. Claude invited them to remain in Brownsville, but he wondered if the danger had followed them. Jacque assured them no one had seen them leave town; they had left in the middle of the night by foot. They had their young daughter with them. Her name was Priscilla, and she was the same age as the twins. Clarissa told the council that Priscilla had gone through a lot emotionally at an early age. She didn't do a lot of talking because she was afraid of people. Priscilla became close friends with the twins. Her parents enrolled her to start school as soon as possible. When she met Randolph, she didn't know he could fly. Claude and the council members didn't believe Jacque had told them the whole story and asked Eyes Eagle's eldest son to watch over the strangers while his father Eyes Eagle was out of town and to also find out the location of the town Jacque had spoken about. The Brown Skins were not used to strangers coming to their village. For years, they had been the only inhabitants, and that caused concern among the council members. They wanted to know about Jacque and Clarissa. The council felt as though Jacque had not revealed all their troubles with them. The council contained elders full of the trials of life and the wisdom that came from those trials. They all agreed more research was needed.

20

Sophia became sick, and her health had begun to fade quickly. She had lost the use of her arms and legs. She was confined to a wheelchair. The next morning, Claude arose to find his mother had passed away peacefully during the night while she was sleeping. Many of her family members paid their last respects once the news circulated through the community. It was hard for Claude and Abigail to accept the fact that she was gone. All he could think about was how he was helpless when his father had passed away several years earlier. Jacque saw all the grief Claude was having and it touched his heart. He and Clarissa came from a generation that didn't have or know how to show compassion, but he was different, which made him an outcast among his kinfolk. He didn't want Priscilla to inherit the danger of his people. The elders wondered among themselves who would make the special tea now that Sophia was gone. Halo remembered how she had secretly watched her great-grandmother make the tea and was sure she could reproduce it. Halo had the same photographic memory as her father, Pierre. She was sure she could prepare it for the festivities. She told Poppa Claude that she hadn't told anyone that she knew the secret formula for the tea. It was secure and would remain with her for the rest of her life. Claude was pleased to know the formula was in good hands for generations to come.

21

This would be Priscilla's and her parents' first festive season with the Brown Skins. The entire village was decorated with an assortment of lights. Eyes and his crew decorated the tallest trees, filling the skyline with a majestic glow that could be seen for miles. Jacque and Clarissa became worried once they were told about the festive season. They knew Priscilla would react differently from the other Brown Skins. She would become overwhelmed with the excitement. They were worried that she would reveal their family secret. When she became excited, her voice would tremble, which was a sign to her parents. They kept Priscilla's secret from everyone because they didn't want her peers to think she was handicapped. Priscilla assured her parents that she would be just fine and she would let them know immediately if she started to feel strange at all with the twins during the ceremonies. She didn't know Randolph had a special surprise for the small kids. He only wished his grandma Sophia would have lived long enough for her to see what he was going to do. As the morning approached on the festive day, most of the children had been up since the rising of the morning sun. Many were showing off their new gifts that were given by the elders. They didn't know about the surprise Randolph had for them; only the elders had knowledge of the surprise. When the evening festivities began, Randolph asked his friends to get the kids to line up in a single file, and his surprise was to give each child a ride on his back while he was flying.

Everyone gathered to see the joy and excitement the children would have. Priscilla and Halo helped the elders with organizing the kids. Priscilla became excited, and her voice was trembling as she spoke, but she told the twins she was okay and not to tell her parents. As Randolph began to fly, Priscilla became more excited. When he took off, she couldn't control her emotions any longer, and within a split second, she was flying too. Everyone was amazed when they saw Priscilla flying. Randolph had never seen anyone else fly except when they drank the tea. One of the elders who saw her immediately went to tell her parents. At first, they acted as though they didn't know what she was doing, but her mother told them she had been flying since the age of two and that's why they had to leave their home. They were accused of practicing witchcraft. The elders said it was foolish for folks to think that way about a child and swore to them that no one would ever say anything like that. Randolph joined Priscilla, and they both laughed and flew off together into the horizon. It was a magical moment for the both of them, and they instantly fell in love. They were gone for days, and everyone began to worry. Eyes sent his crew to search for them, but they weren't anywhere to be found. The fish told Eyes that he and some of the others were scouting the shoreline and saw them fly out to the big water, but he hadn't seen them return. He told them that they shouldn't worry because he could see they were in love and were having a great time together. They all gazed into the stars, waiting to catch a glimpse of their new couple, but what they saw were green flashes across the sky. Eyes thought it may have been a storm approaching, but Claude didn't agree. Paul hadn't seen those before, and he had lived there the longest. They all figured that Randolph and Priscilla would return soon, and they went back to their homes and waited for them to return. Weeks had passed without a sign of Randolph and Priscilla. Claude refused to give up hope of finding his grandson. He and a crew he put together with Paul Bear searched, sunup to sundown. His only other option was the big water and risking going back north. He knew it would take weeks to continue the search on foot. He asked Halo to prepare enough of the special tea that would allow this search party to fly across the big water and make a return trip back to the south. Halo told him it would take her several days because it would be her first batch. Claude agreed and scheduled the search to begin in seventy-two hours. The team met at the entrance of the big water that flowed through the north side of the ice mountain. Jacque and Clarissa came also. Jacque demanded to be a part of the search team because Priscilla was his daughter. As the team lifted off to cross the big water, they were cheered on by the crowd that had gathered. Claude swore to Abigail he would not return without Randolph. He had lost his son, and he refused to lose his only grandson. The crew took flight across the big water, and the search began.

To be continued...

ABOUT THE AUTHOR

E ric was born on October 8, 1960 and raised in Virginia. Eric was very active as a child with an incredible imagination! He also loved to play sports but excelled mostly in football until he was injured. As he grew into a young adult, Eric joined the United States Marine Corps with three of his best friends, after he served in the Marines his first daughter was born. He has three daughters, Alicia, Alexandria, and Andria, and a granddaughter, Halo.

Growing up on a farm, Eric read books and built model cars, but he soon discovered that writing was his passion. It was his destiny. With encouragement from his sister and youngest daughter, Andria, Eric decided it was time to bring his writings to life. Randolph was born.

Created from his imagination and love for Christmas, Eric hopes Randolph will be the first of many publications in the future. He dedicates this book to his late mother, Edith Baker Copeland, and his granddaughter, Halo.

Printed in the USA
CPSIA information can be obtained
at www.ICGtesting.com
CBHW041116171024
15895CB00027BA/227/J